S0-EAW-776

EAGLE VALLEY LIBRARY DISTRICT
1 06 0003689999

PowerKids Readers:

The Bilingual Library of the United States of America™

Bilingual Edition
English/Spanish
Edición bilingüe

PENNSYLVANIA

PENSILVANIA

JENNIFER WAY

TRADUCCIÓN AL ESPAÑOL: MARÍA CRISTINA BRUSCA

The Rosen Publishing Group's
PowerKids Press™ & Editorial Buenas Letras™
New York

Published in 2006 by The Rosen Publishing Group, Inc.
29 East 21st Street, New York, NY 10010

First Edition

Photo Credits: Cover © Michael P. Gadomski/Superstock; p. 5 © Joseph Sohm; ChromoSohm Inc./Corbis; p. 7 © 2002 Geoatlas; pp. 9, 31 (Hills) © Ross M. Horowitz/Getty Images; pp. 11, 31 (Alcott, Carson) © Bettmann/Corbis; p. 13 © Lester Lefkowitz/Corbis; p. 15 © Getty Images; pp. 17, 31 (Buchanan, Battle) © Corbis; pp. 19, 25, 30 (Capital) © Richard T. Nowitz/Corbis; p. 21 © Jason Cohn/Reuters/Corbis; p. 23 © Gary Randall/Getty Images; pp. 26, 30 (Eastern Hemlock) © Gary Braasch/Corbis; p. 30 (Mountain Laurel) © Hal Horwitz/Corbis; p. 30 (Ruffed Grouse) © Tom Brakefield/Corbis; p. 31 (Franklin) © The Corcoran Gallery of Art/Corbis; p. 31 (Cassatt) Library of Congress Prints and Photographs Division; p. 31 (Cosby) © Lynn Goldsmith/Corbis

Library of Congress Cataloging-in-Publication Data

Way, Jennifer.
Pennsylvania / Jennifer Way ; traducción al español, María Cristina Brusca. — 1st ed.
p. cm. — (The bilingual library of the United States of America)
Includes bibliographical references and index.
ISBN 1-4042-3103-X (library binding)
1. Pennsylvania—Juvenile literature. I. Title. II. Series.
F149.3.W39 2006
974.8—dc22

2005026671

Manufactured in the United States of America

Due to the changing nature of Internet links, Editorial Buenas Letras has developed an online list of Web sites related to the subject of this book. This site is updated regularly. Please use this link to access the list:

http://www.buenasletraslinks.com/ls/pennsylvania

Contents

Contenido

Welcome to Pennsylvania

Pennsylvania is known as the Keystone State. A keystone holds an arch in place. The nickname means that Pennsylvania is important to the founding of the United States.

Bienvenidos a Pensilvania

Pensilvania es conocido como el Estado Piedra Clave. La piedra clave es el punto que mantiene unido a un arco. Esto nos recuerda que Pensilvania fue importante en la fundación de los Estados Unidos.

Pennsylvania Flag and State Seal

Bandera y escudo de Pensilvania

Pennsylvania Geography

Pennsylvania borders the states of Delaware, Maryland, New Jersey, New York, Ohio and West Virginia. Pennsylvania also borders Lake Erie, which is one of the five Great Lakes.

Geografía de Pensilvania

Pensilvania linda con los estados de Delaware, Maryland, Nueva Jersey, Nueva York, Ohio y Virginia Occidental. Pensilvania también linda con el lago Erie, que es uno de los cinco Grandes Lagos.

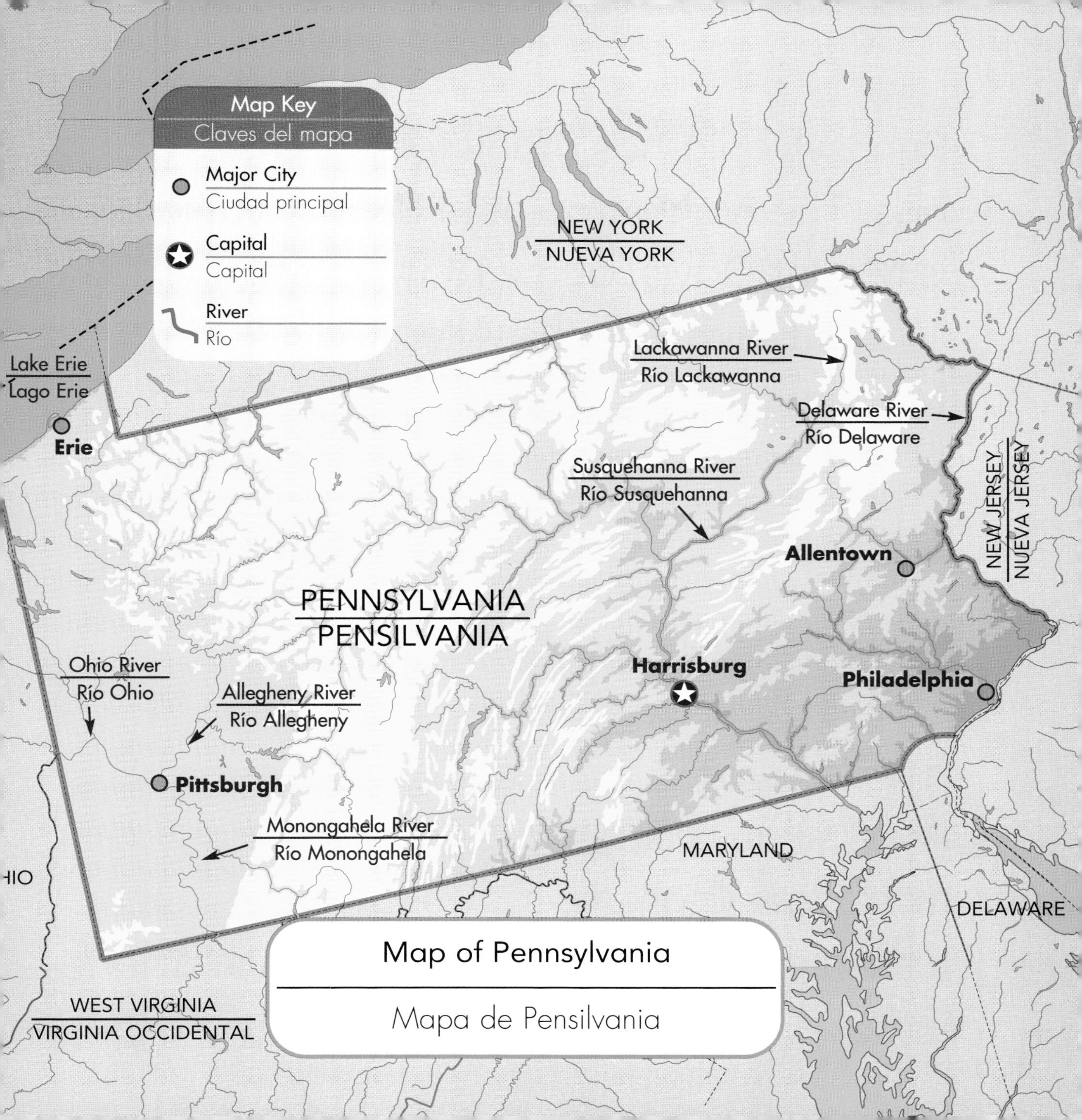
Map Key
Claves del mapa
Major City
Ciudad principal
Capital
Capital
River
Río
NEW YORK
NUEVA YORK
Lake Erie
Lago Erie
Erie
Lackawanna River
Río Lackawanna
Delaware River
Río Delaware
Susquehanna River
Río Susquehanna
NEW JERSEY
NUEVA JERSEY
Allentown
PENNSYLVANIA
PENSILVANIA
Ohio River
Río Ohio
Allegheny River
Río Allegheny
Harrisburg
Philadelphia
Pittsburgh
Monongahela River
Río Monongahela
MARYLAND
HIO
DELAWARE
WEST VIRGINIA
VIRGINIA OCCIDENTAL

Map of Pennsylvania

Mapa de Pensilvania

Pennsylvania has many forests and hills. The highest point in Pennsylvania is Mount Davis, at 3,213 ft (979 m). Mount Davis is in the Allegheny Mountains. The Alleghenies are part of the Appalachian Mountains.

Pensilvania tiene muchos bosques y colinas. El monte Davis es el punto más alto de Pensilvania. Tiene 3,213 pies (979 m) de altura y se encuentra en las montañas Allegheny. Las Alleghenies forman parte de las montañas Apalaches.

Fall in the Allegheny Mountains

Otoño en las montañas Allegheny

Pennsylvania History

William Penn founded Pennsylvania in 1682. Penn was a Quaker. Quakers believe in freedom of faith. Freedom of faith is an important idea to the United States.

Historia de Pensilvania

William Penn fundó Pensilvania en 1682. Penn seguía la religión llamada Cuaquerismo. Los cuáqueros creen en la libertad religiosa. Ésta es una idea importante para los Estados Unidos.

William Penn (1644–1718)

The Declaration of Independence was signed in Independence Hall in Philadelphia, in 1776. This document said that the colonies wanted to break away from Great Britain. When the declaration was first read in public, the Liberty Bell was rung.

La Declaración de Independencia fue firmada en el Salón de la Independencia, en Filadelfia, en 1776. Este documento decía que las colonias querían separarse de Gran Bretaña. Cuando se leyó la declaración de independencia, se hizo sonar la Campana de la Libertad.

Independence Hall and the Liberty Bell

El Salón de la Independencia y la Campana de la Libertad

Philadelphia was the capital of the United States from 1790 until 1800. Some of the city's buildings were used by Congress, the Supreme Court and the president. In 1800, the U.S. capital was moved to Washington, D.C.

Filadelfia fue la capital de los Estados Unidos de 1790 a 1800. El congreso, la suprema corte y el presidente utilizaron varios de los edificios de la ciudad. En 1800, la capital se trasladó a Washington, D.C.

Congress Hall in Philadelphia

Edificio del congreso en Filadelfia

The Battle of Gettysburg was the biggest battle of the Civil War. The war was fought from 1861 to 1865 between the North and the South. More than 50,000 people were killed in the Battle of Gettysburg.

La batalla de Gettysburg fue la más grande de la Guerra Civil. Esta guerra, entre el Norte y el Sur, se peleó de 1861 a 1865. En la batalla de Gettysburg murieron más de 50,000 personas.

Battle of Gettysburg, July 1863

Batalla de Gettysburg, julio de 1863

Living in Pennsylvania

Many Pennsylvanians are proud of their state's history. Some people dress up in historical clothing to help teach others about Pennsylvania's history.

La vida en Pensilvania

Muchos pensilvanos están orgullosos de la historia de su estado. Algunos de ellos visten ropas históricas para poder enseñar a otros acerca de la historia de Pensilvania.

Pennsylvanians Acting Out the Battle of Gettysburg

Pensilvanos en una recreación de la batalla de Gettysburg

Punxsutawney, Pennsylvania, is famous for Groundhog Day. Every February a groundhog named Phil comes out of his hole. If Phil sees his shadow, the story says, there will be six more weeks of winter. If he does not see it, spring is on the way.

Punxsutawney, Pensilvania, es famosa por su Día de la Marmota. Cada febrero, una marmota llamada Phil sale de su cueva. La leyenda dice que si Phil ve su sombra quedan seis semanas de invierno. Si no ve su sombra, la primavera llegará pronto.

Groundhog Day in Punxsutawney, Pennsylvania

Día de la Marmota en Punxsutawney, Pensilvania

The city of Pittsburgh is in western Pennsylvania. Three rivers meet in the city. These are the Ohio River, the Allegheny River and the Monongahela River.

La ciudad de Pittsburgh está en la zona oeste de Pensilvania. Tres ríos se encuentran en la ciudad. Estos son el río Ohio, el río Allegheny y el río Monongahela.

Pittsburgh, Pennsylvania

Pittsburgh, Pensilvania

Philadelphia, Pittsburgh, and Allentown are the biggest cities in Pennsylvania. Harrisburg is the capital of the state of Pennsylvania.

Filadelfia, Pittsburgh y Allentown son las ciudades más grandes de Pensilvania. Harrisburg es la capital del estado de Pensilvania.

Pennsylvania Capitol Building in Harrisburg

Capitolio de Pensilvania en Harrisburg

Activity:
Let´s Draw Pennsylvania's State Tree

The Eastern Hemlock Is Pennsylvania's State Tree

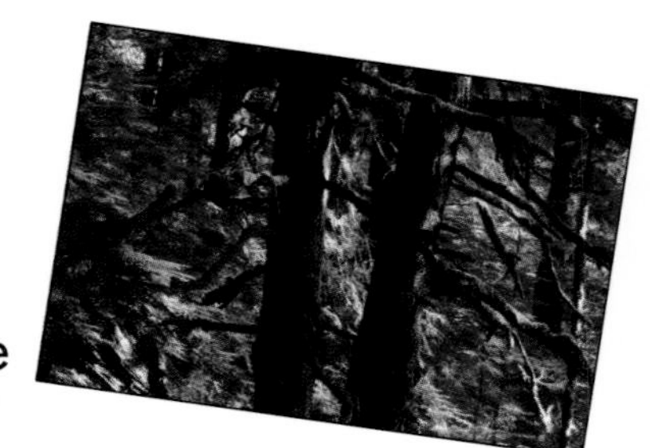

Actividad:
Dibujemos el árbol del estado de Pensilvania

La cicuta oriental es el árbol del estado de Pensilvania

1

Draw three lines as shown. This is the trunk of the tree.

Dibuja tres líneas verticales. Éste es el tronco de tu árbol.

2

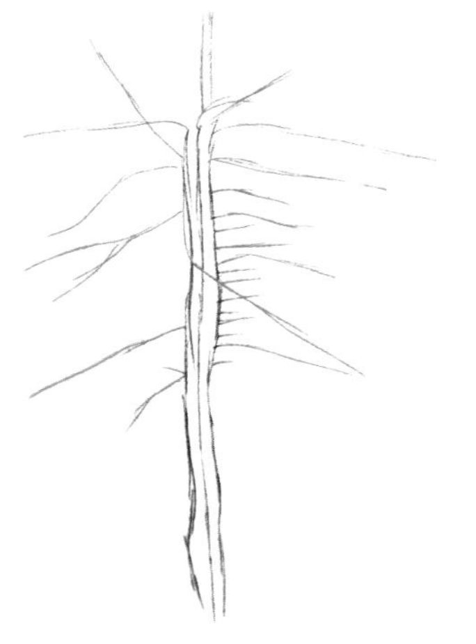

Draw lines that come out from the trunk. These are the branches.

Dibuja líneas que salgan del tronco. Éstas son las ramas.

3

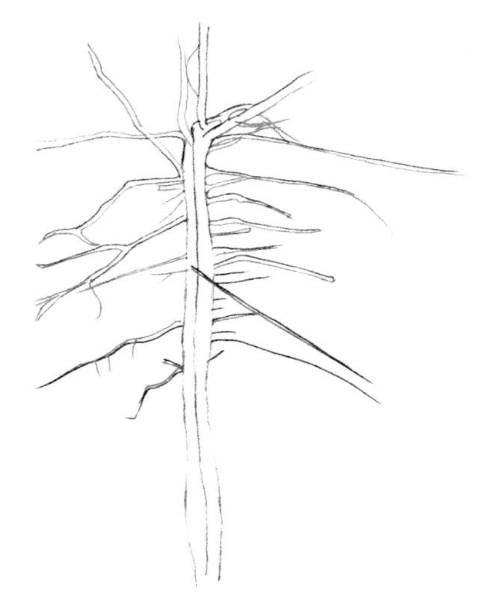

To make the branches thicker, draw other lines next to the first ones you drew for all the branches.

Para que las ramas se vean más gruesas traza otras líneas al lado de las que ya has trazado cuando dibujaste las ramas.

4

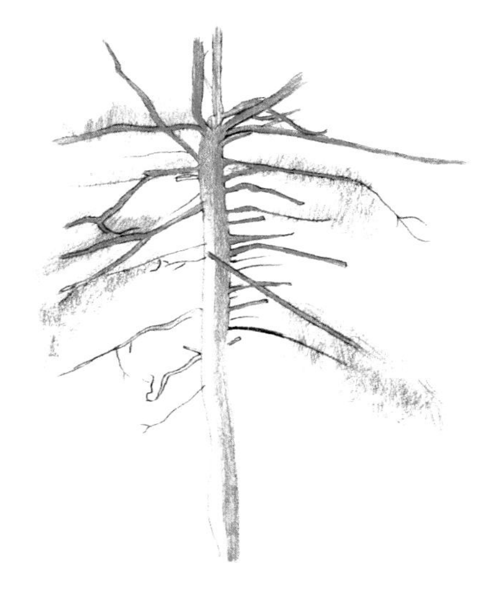

Shade in the drawing. Turn your pencil on its side and gently shade.

Sombrea el dibujo. Apoya tu lápiz de costado y sombrea con suavidad.

Timeline		Cronología
William Penn founds the Pennsylvania Colony.	1682	William Penn funda la Colonia de Pensilvania.
The Declaration of Independence is signed in Philadelphia.	1776	Se firma la Declaración de Independencia en Filadelfia.
Pennsylvania becomes the second state to join the United States.	1787	Pensilvania es el segundo estado en unirse a los Estados Unidos.
Philadelphia is the capital of the United States. Washington, D.C. becomes the capital in 1800.	1790	Filadelfia es la capital de los Estados Unidos. En 1800 la capital se traslada a Washington.
The Battle of Gettysburg is fought in the Civil War.	1863	Se lleva al cabo la batalla de Gettysburg durante la Guerra Civil.
America's first radio station is begun in Pittsburgh.	1920	En Pittsburgh se crea la primera emisora de radio de los Estados Unidos.
Dr. Jonas Salk creates the first vaccine for polio at the University of Pittsburgh Medical School.	1947	El Dr. Jonas Salk descubre la primera vacuna para la polio en la Universidad de Medicina de Pittsburgh.
The Andy Warhol Museum opens in the artist's hometown, Pittsburgh.	1994	Se inaugura el Museo Andy Warhol en la ciudad natal del artista, Pittsburgh.

Pennsylvania Events

January
Mummers Day Parade, Philadelphia

February
Groundhog Day, Punxsutawney

May
Apple Blossom Festival, Gettysburg

June
Generoo Arts Festival, Beaver Springs
Gettysburg Civil War Days, Gettysburg

July
Adams County Irish Festival, Gettysburg
German Festival, Kutztown

August
Endless Mountains Blues Fest, Elmhurst

September
Puerto Rican Day Parade, Philadelphia

October
Green Tree Oktoberfest, Pittsburgh
Black Bear Film Festival, Milford

Eventos en Pensilvania

Enero
Desfile de los Enmascarados, en Filadelfia

Febrero
Día de la Marmota, en Punxsutawney

Mayo
Festival de la flor del manzano, en Gettysburg

Junio
Festival artístico Generoo, en Beaver Springs
Días de la Guerra Civil, en Gettysburg

Julio
Festival irlandés del condado de Adams, en Gettysburg
Festival alemán, en Kutztown

Agosto
Festival de *blues* de las montañas, en Elmhurst

Septiembre
Desfile del Día de Puerto Rico, en Filadelfia

Octubre
Oktoberfest en Pittsburgh
Festival de cine Black Bear, en Milford

Pennsylvania Facts/Datos sobre Pensilvania

Population
12.3 million

Población
12.3 millones

Capital
Harrisburg

Capital
Harrisburg

State Motto
Virtue, Liberty, and Independence

Lema del estado
Virtud, Libertad e Independencia

State Flower
Mountain laurel

Flor del estado
Laurel de montaña

State Bird
Ruffed grouse

Ave del estado
Grévol engolado

State Nickname
The Keystone State

Mote del estado
El Estado Piedra Clave

State Tree
Eastern hemlock

Árbol del estado
Cicuta oriental

State Song
"Pennsylvania"

Canción del estado
"Pensilvania"

Famous Pennsylvanians/Pensilvanos famosos

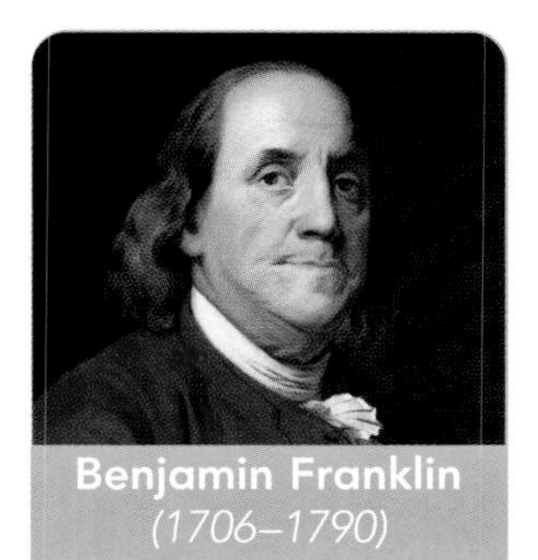

Benjamin Franklin
(1706–1790)
Inventor and diplomat
Inventor y diplomático

James Buchanan
(1791–1868)
U.S. president
Presidente de E.U.A.

Louisa May Alcott
(1832–1888)
Writer
Escritora

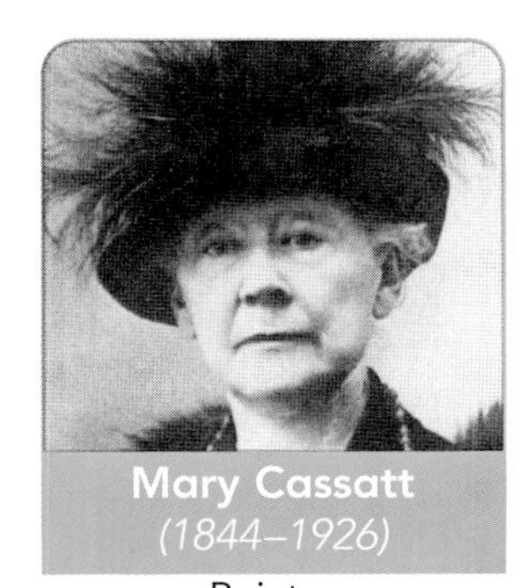

Mary Cassatt
(1844–1926)
Painter
Pintora

Bill Cosby
(1937–)
Comedian
Comediante

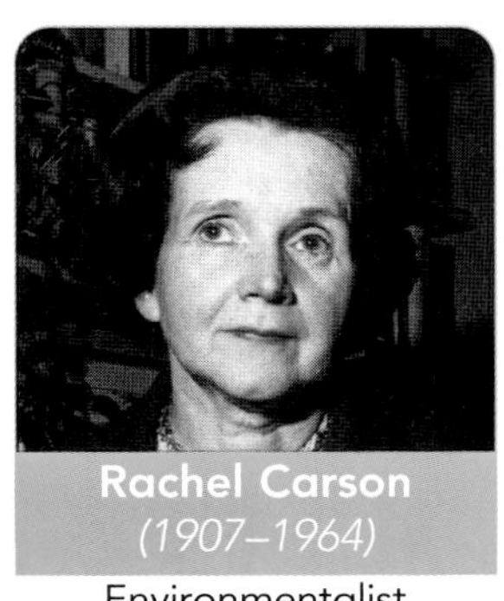

Rachel Carson
(1907–1964)
Environmentalist
Ambientalista

Words to Know/Palabras que debes saber

battle
batalla

border
frontera

hills
colinas

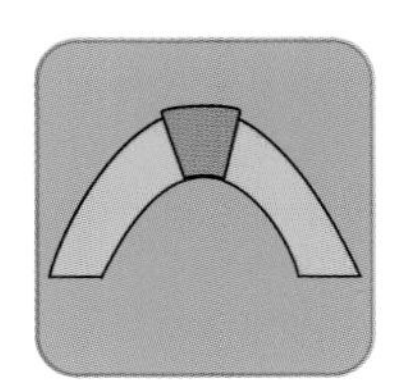

arch
arco

Here are more books to read about Pennsylvania:
Otros libros que puedes leer sobre Pensilvania:

In English/En inglés:

Pennsylvania Facts and Activities
by Carole Marsh
Gallopade International, 1996

Pennsylvania
by Kathleen Thompson
Steck-Vaughn, 1996

Words in English: 342

Palabras en español: 365

Index

Índice